Beast Quest®

KYRAX
THE METAL WARRIOR

BY ADAM BLADE

ORCHARD

FORESTED SINKHOLE

HENKRALL

GREAT NORTHERN MARKET

GEYSER ISLAND

CONTENTS

STORY ONE

THE BIRTH OF A BEAST

*Things get boring in Avantia sometimes –
so boring, I occasionally have to come here,
to the Pickpocket's Purse, to play dice and
make some extra money. Not that I really
care about money, of course – I just like to
see the embarrassed look on the faces of
the stupid men when I beat them over and
over again. They get so angry!*

*But as fun as this is, I can't help craving
a bit more excitement. Maybe Tom and
Elenna will get sent on a Quest soon, and
need some help. That does not mean I
really care what happens to them on their
adventures – I'm just very, very bored.
That's all!*

*And it probably won't be long now.
Because if there's one thing I know for
sure, it's this: in Avantia, danger is never
far away.*

Yours, very bored,

Petra the witch

AN UNLIKELY STORY

Captain Harkman frowned as he examined the newly forged sword. At Tom's side, his uncle Henry craned forwards, hardly breathing. Elenna shuffled her feet. The clink of iron on steel echoed through the palace courtyard, and smoke from the forge hung thick in the morning air.

"Hmm…" Harkman rubbed his chin.

Tom's uncle had been drafted in to oversee the manufacture of new arms for the king's soldiers. As a master blacksmith, Henry's work was renowned throughout Avantia – but Harkman was a hard man to please.

Finally, the captain lifted his eyes from the blade. They twinkled. "Remarkable," he said. "I've never seen such a fine weapon."

Henry grinned. "It is an honour to serve the king," he said.

Tom rolled his eyes. "That's all very well," he said. "But what about Storm? He really needs his new shoes."

Henry shot Tom a playful scowl. "Storm won't go without, you know that," he said.

The sudden clatter of hoofbeats grabbed Tom's attention.

"Make way!" a screechy voice cried. Tom turned to see a chestnut mare thunder through the courtyard gates. It pulled up in a cloud of dust, its flanks heaving. A portly man with a feathered velvet cap leapt from its saddle. A few moments later, a cart pulled by a pair of scrawny donkeys rattled into the courtyard.

"Which way to the dungeons?" the man cried. A slender youth in red and gold livery pulled the donkeys to a halt. Three broad men were huddled in the back of the cart, bound and gagged. Grey dust covered their weathered skin and clothes, but their eyes blazed with fury.

Harkman crossed the courtyard
in long strides. "I am Captain of the
King's Guards. What's going on?"

"These men are thieves!" the capped
man replied. "I own the Rocky Gold
Mine up in the Northern Mountains.
They work my mine. I foolishly
trusted them to deliver my gold, but

instead they stole it."

Muffled cries and the stamp of boots erupted from the back of the cart. The three men waved their bound wrists, their eyes bulging above their gags as they tried to shout.

Harkman lifted a hand. "Wait!" he said. "I'll not lock men up without hearing both sides of the tale." He strode to the cart, tugged a knife from his belt, and cut the men's gags free.

All three started talking at once. Tom caught the words 'spears' and 'attack', before Harkman clapped his hands. "One at a time!"

The miners fell silent; then the oldest, a man with fierce blue eyes and greying whiskers, nodded to Harkman. "We are no thieves," he said. "On our way to deliver the gold, we were attacked and our cargo was stolen. We had no chance against our attackers – there were too many of them, and..." The man paused, looking down at his tied hands.

"Go on," Harkman said.

The man gritted his teeth. "They

had wings. They came on us from the sky and drove us from our cart with spears and swords. When we returned, they'd taken everything."

"Lies!" the mine owner cried, stamping his foot. Tom and Elenna exchanged a look.

"Henkrall," Elenna mouthed.

Tom nodded. They had visited the strange kingdom many Quests ago. In Henkrall, all creatures, even humans, had wings. The Evil Witch Kensa had been banished there once. She had escaped – but still, Tom couldn't help wondering if she might be behind this attack.

"Captain," Tom murmured, "it is possible these men speak the truth. The attackers they describe sound

like warriors from Henkrall. Until we
know the full story, I think we should
trust their word." Tom ran his eyes
over the men's cracked lips and filthy
clothes. "Food and a bath for the men,
and a stable for those poor animals
would be a start," he said.

Harkman gave a nod. "Aye," he said. "I suppose that's fair."

The merchant before him let out an angry splutter. "Surely you can't—"

Harkman lifted his hand, cutting the man off. "If it turns out they're lying, they'll face the king's justice. Until then, they are our guests."

Suddenly a furious scream rang out from above – high, wild and filled with rage.

"The queen's in trouble!" Elenna cried.

"Get out this instant!" Aroha's shouts echoed down from her tower window. Tom heard a crash and the sound of splintering glass.

THIEVES FROM THE SKY

Tom could hear grunts and the clash of weapons as he pounded up the spiral stairs, using the speed from his golden boots. The magical armour of the Master of the Beasts was safe in the palace armoury, but Tom could still use its magic.

"Aroha, I'm coming!" King Hugo shouted from far below.

Tom reached the door to Aroha's room and flung it wide. Inside he found Aroha swiping a golden sceptre at a winged young man bearing down on her from above. The queen's sleeve was torn and a long cut ran above one eyebrow, but her green eyes flashed with fury. *Thud!* She landed a hefty blow across the side of her attacker's head. The man's wingbeats faltered and he sank to the ground, unconscious. Three more burly winged men crowded forward, armed with long spears and carrying bulging sacks over their shoulders.

Tom lunged towards the nearest, swinging his sword. The man flapped back out of reach. Tom sprang after him, but the winged man turned and

dived through the open tower window.
Tom caught a flash of movement from
the corner of his eye. He spun and
flicked his sword to deflect a vicious
spear-thrust from another attacker.
The man barged past and leapt
through the window after his friend.

"Don't touch that!" Aroha shrieked.

Tom looked to see her raining blows
down on the back of the third man
while he shoved the helmet of her
rose gold armour into his sack. The
man thrust the queen away, spread
his wings and flapped towards the
window.

King Hugo burst into the room with
Elenna. "They're escaping!" he cried.

Tom lunged towards the final
warrior as he dived through the tower

window, just managing to catch hold
of the man's ankle.

"Whoa!" Tom's stomach lurched
as he was yanked from the room by
his arms and dragged out over the
palace courtyard. The winged soldier
plummeted under the sudden strain

of Tom's weight. Tom winced, his muscles clenching in fear as they plunged towards the cobbles. The warrior flapped hard and Tom drew a shuddering breath as they levelled.

"Let go!" the thief cried, shaking his leg. Tom kept his hands locked tight about the man's ankle, and peered into the wind. He could see the dark silhouettes of the two other men, far ahead. A glowing speck appeared in the sky before them, quickly swelling and brightening.

A portal! Tom realised. *They're going to escape!*

The winged man kicked his free leg at Tom's face. Tom ducked his head sideways, dodging the blow, but the man kicked again. The heel of his boot cracked down on Tom's shoulder.

"Aargh!" Pain fizzed down Tom's arm. He lost his grip and tumbled free. Wind sped past and hard grey stone rushed up to meet him.

He threw his shield up, calling on the power of Arcta the Mountain Giant's eagle feather. With a jolt that clashed his teeth together, he slowed – but not enough. The cobbles raced past in a blur. Tom tipped his shield, using it like a sail, angling his fall towards a pile of hay near the stables.

Whump! He plunged deep into the springy heap. He shoved the biting stalks aside, digging himself from the hay, then skidded down the side of the mound. As he brushed hay from his hair and clothes, he saw Elenna racing

towards him across the courtyard.

"Are you all right?" she called.

"I think so…" Tom shouted back.

"Then let's get those thieves!"
Elenna tugged open the stable doors
and Tom ducked in after her. Storm
lifted his head and greeted them with
a neigh. Tom leapt on to his horse's
back. Elenna vaulted up behind him.

With a tap of Tom's heels, Storm
surged forwards across the courtyard,
though the gates and out on to the
open road.

Elenna pointed ahead. "There!"

Tom spotted the attackers flying
hard and fast towards the portal.
Storm's hooves thundered, kicking up
dust. But even as he urged his horse
onwards, Tom knew it was useless.

We'll never catch them!

The first warrior reached the portal and vanished with a flash of light. The second followed an instant later. Frustration swelled in Tom's chest as the third and final man disappeared. Tom pulled Storm to a stop.

"You did your best," Elenna said.

Tom watched the spot of light in the sky dwindle to nothing. He heaved a sigh and turned to his friend. "It wasn't good enough," he said. "But while there's blood in my veins, I'll catch those thieves."

THE PICKPOCKET'S PURSE

Tom walked slowly, his eyes on the flagstones as he and Elenna made their way to King Hugo's throne room. Inside, he found Hugo and Aroha seated, bathed in light from the stained glass windows behind them. A light bandage covered the queen's forehead. Daltec and Aduro stood beside the king, watching Tom expectantly.

Tom bowed his head. As he lifted his gaze to the king and queen, he could feel his face burning with shame. "The thieves escaped through a portal in the sky, taking all they had stolen with them," he said. "I've failed you."

Hugo shook his head. "Tom, don't be so hard on yourself. You acted with honour and bravery. The most important thing is that you may just have saved the queen's life by arriving as quickly as you did." Hugo turned to Aroha with an exasperated frown. "I don't know what you were thinking, taking on four armed men by yourself."

Aroha arched an eyebrow. "Must I remind you that the queens of Tangala have always been warriors? I was hardly going to sit there like some helpless damsel in distress while they ransacked my possessions."

Hurried boots sounded outside the chamber door and Hugo turned towards them with a look of relief.

Captain Harkman stormed in, dragging a dark-haired youth with a pair of huge feathered wings jutting from his back. The boy looked barely older than Tom, and his knees shook as Harkman thrust him further into the room. Tom noticed an egg-shaped purple bruise on the boy's forehead from where Aroha had struck him.

"What were you doing? Tom demanded of the youth. "I don't remember the warriors of Henkrall being common thieves."

The boy flinched at Tom's words. "We

aren't," he said. "Well, we *weren't*. But
our new leader sends us on raids to
other kingdoms, to take any precious
metal we can find. If we don't bring
back enough, we don't eat. Neither do
our families. We have no choice."

New leader? Tom thought. *Could
that be Kensa?*

Daltec frowned. "What's all the metal for?" he asked.

"I don't know, sir," the boy said. He twisted his hands together. "No one does... Please let me go. I want to go home. My mother will be so worried."

"I'd send you home if I could," Daltec said. "But the portal's closed. There is no way back to Henkrall."

The boy's shoulders drooped. Tom felt a stab of pity. He thought of his last dangerous journey to Henkrall.

"There's the Lightning Path," he said.

Aduro shook his head fiercely. "Don't even think of it! Must I remind you that it was the unauthorised use of the Lightning Staff that got me expelled from the Circle of Wizards? Even if they would give us access to the staff

– which they won't – I don't want Daltec enduring the same fate."

Daltec put a hand on Aduro's sleeve. "Master, I think I know a way to get our hands on the staff," he said.

Aduro's frown deepened. "It would be madness to go against the circle's wishes – not to mention the danger of using such powerful sorcery."

"True," Daltec said, tipping his head. "But, madness or not, I think I know someone who might help us out. If only because she likes to show off…" Daltec grinned at Tom.

Elenna groaned. "You have to be joking," she said.

Tom shot her a puzzled frown. "What do you mean? Whoever Daltec knows, surely we must try them. It might be our only way of getting to the bottom of this mystery."

Elenna gaped at Tom, then shook her head and let out a sigh that was more like a growl. "Fine," she said. "Just don't say I didn't warn you."

Flickering torchlight reflected from the filthy puddles at Tom's feet and glistened along the slimy brickwork as he and Elenna hurried past. Tom knew that, somewhere above, the moon shone bright — but here, high, crooked walls kept the narrow alleyway locked in gloom. Tom pulled his scratchy hood lower over his face. A rasping snore rose from the dark alcove nearby. Tom peered into the shadows to see a man sprawled there.

Ahead, a door banged open, spilling a rectangle of yellow light across the dark cobblestones. Rowdy singing blasted out into the night along with the clink of glasses. A cloaked figure lurched through the doorway, then tottered away down the alley, cursing loudly each time he slammed into a wall. The door banged shut, cutting off the noise.

"We're really going in there?" Elenna whispered.

"I'm afraid so," Tom said. He would rather face a Beast than set foot in the Pickpocket's Purse – but they had no choice if they wanted to get the queen's belongings back.

He crossed to the door and shoved

it open. As his eyes adjusted to the smoke-filled gloom, he saw crooked beams and crowded tables surrounded by hunched figures nursing tankards of ale. A high wooden counter separated shelves of dusty bottles from the rest of the room. A low fire smouldered in one corner. The jingle of coins mingled with the growled laughter and rough voices. Tom took in the patrons' tattooed arms and grizzled beards with growing unease. He longed for the reassuring weight of his sword. But, as he and Elenna had come in disguise, they had left their bulky weapons behind.

"Ha!" a deep voice crowed from nearby. "I've got you now! Only a double six will do."

Three huge men leaned over a table, peering at a pair of bone dice. One was grinning, showing a mix of black and gold teeth. A smaller figure sat opposite him, dark eyes glinting from under a low, grime-covered hood. A huge pile of coins glittered in the middle of the table. The hooded figure shot out a slender hand, scooped the dice up, then cast them. The three big men craned closer as the dice tumbled. The first dice landed. A six. Then the other came to rest. Tom spotted a three. The gold-toothed man gave a whoop of triumph, but it turned to an angry roar as the dice jiggled and toppled over. Another six.

The hooded figure let out a cackle

and leaned over the table, scooping
the coins into an open purse. "Bad
luck, boys!" a girl's voice cried.

"Typical," Elenna muttered.

Tom nodded. They had found who
they were looking for.

INSIDE THE CIRCLE

Angry shouts erupted from around the table. Tom stood poised near the doorway with Elenna beside him. The gold-toothed man shot to his feet, sending his chair flying. He shoved his big head over the table and peered hard at the hooded figure's shadowed face. Then he let out an angry roar, grabbed her hood and threw it back.

Petra's greasy hair spilled free. She grinned at the man.

"I know this girl!" the man snarled. "She's a witch! No wonder the dice always fell her way. Stinking cheat!" He grabbed the edge of the table and tossed it over.

Petra leapt back, flashing the men a broad smile. "Thanks for the game," she said, "but I must be off. This money won't spend itself!" Petra darted towards the door, her cloak flaring as she dodged through the crowded room. The men charged after her, shoving tables aside, knives glinting in their fists.

Petra shot past Tom and out into the night. The three big men piled after her. Tom stuck out his foot, making

the first man topple. The second
pulled up quickly, but the third
slammed into his back, throwing him
on top of the first. Tom leapt over
their fallen bodies and dived out into
the cool alleyway with Elenna on his
heels. Angry shouts echoed behind
them. Tom put on a burst of speed
and sprang forwards, snatching the
hem of the witch's cloak.

She skidded to a stop then spun
to face him, her eyes flashing and
her hands raised. Magical energy
crackled between her palms.

"Oh, it's you!" she said, her hands
falling. "Do you mind? I've three very
good reasons to get out of here fast!"

"I need your help," Tom said.

Petra scowled, eyeing him

suspiciously. "What do you want? I'm not going off on any ludicrous suicide missions, if that's what you're after."

"No," Tom said. "We just need you to borrow something for us. From, um… the Circle of Wizards."

"Well, I can't help you with that, either," Petra snapped.

Tom could hear the thud of running feet along with angry grunts getting closer by the moment.

"Oh, I think you can," Elenna said. "Daltec told us you were invited to join the circle just a few days ago for helping us stop Jezrin. Apparently you jumped at the chance – which is odd, because I seem to remember you saying you had no time for those old 'fuddy-duddies and their silly club'."

Petra hitched her chin. "I don't,"
she said, "but if they want to give
me access to loads of powerful new
spells just for keeping you two out of
trouble, then who am I to argue?"

"Hypocrite," Elenna muttered.

Petra fixed her with a blank-
eyed stare. "You've got a funny way
of asking for help," she said. "Why
would I ever risk my neck for you two
again?"

The thud and splash of boots was
almost on them now. "The little cheat
can't have got far," a gruff voice cried.
"Let's try that way."

Petra rolled her eyes at Tom. "This
is getting boring," she said. Then she
flashed him her familiar wicked grin.
"I quite fancy a Quest now!"

"There they are!" a man shouted. Tom turned to see three huge figures turn the corner and lumber towards them.

He balled his fists. "Let's go, then!"

Petra laughed. "One doesn't 'go' to the circle. It comes to you." She lifted her hands and muttered a few strange words. The three men leapt towards them, their faces twisted into cruel scowls. Just as they made to lunge, though, the air shimmered and a plain wooden door appeared, blocking them from sight. Petra pulled the door open, and stepped through. Tom and Elenna leapt after her.

The door slammed shut with an echoing thud. Tom glanced about, his heart hammering. He found himself in a long, silent corridor with a shining

marble floor. Elegantly carved pillars reached to a vaulted ceiling above. What looked like hundreds of identical wooden doors ran down either side of the corridor.

Petra strode off, her footsteps echoing in the stillness. Tom and Elenna followed. Passageways led away on either side of them, all spotless shining marble lined with simple wooden doors. Petra passed most of the doors without a second glance; but at some, she stopped and peered hard at the wood. Each time, she shook her head and moved on. Tom and Elenna followed her through the maze of doors, turning corner after corner until Tom had no idea which way they had come. As he watched Petra pacing calmly ahead of them, he started to feel uneasy.

Is she leading us on?

He couldn't stand it any longer. "Where are we going?" he asked.

"The Lightning Staff is behind one of these doors," Petra said. "I have to find the right one. The other doors mostly lead to witches and wizards in different kingdoms. I don't want to go bursting in on them. That would be dangerous. Not to mention highly embarrassing."

"Wouldn't it be simpler to just find a door that leads to Henkrall?" Elenna asked.

Petra shook her head. "As far as I know, there aren't any sorcerers in Henkrall. Which means there's no door." She pulled up suddenly and lifted a hand, frowning hard at a smooth, polished door. "I think this is the one," she said.

"You *think*?" Elenna asked.

"I don't know if you've noticed, but all these doors look quite similar. This is my best guess. Take it or leave it."

Elenna's eyes narrowed. Tom took a deep breath, reached out a hand towards the door that Petra had chosen. Then he pushed.

It opened into a small stone room, not much bigger than a wardrobe, and empty but for a simple wooden stand. Resting in the stand, like a discarded walking stick, stood the Lightning Staff.

"You did it!" Tom said, striding

forwards. Intricate symbols covered the silvery metal of the staff. Tom reached out and gripped the handle.

BONG! BONG! BONG! Tom clapped his hands over his ears. A sound like a thousand bells all ringing at once boomed around him.

"A magical alarm," said Petra. "We'd better get out of here, now!"

A PEOPLE ENSLAVED

Tom snatched up the staff and sped from the room, the clang of bells loud in his ears.

"This way!" Petra cried, pointing down a long corridor. Doors flew open ahead of them. Cloaked figures, tall and short, old and young, bundled through, fixing their eyes on the staff in Tom's hand.

"Stop them!" a balding, overstuffed wizard cried, his jowls wobbling with rage.

"Thief!" a tall witch with jet black hair screeched, her amber eyes blazing as she pointed at Tom.

"Follow me!" Petra called, waving her hands and firing bolts of blue energy.

The witches and wizards leapt aside, clearing a path. Petra set her jaw and ran. Tom raced after her

with Elenna close at his heels. A woman with flaming red hair and a green cloak leapt into Tom's path. He dodged sideways, then ducked past a youth with glowing purple eyes. Petra's cloak streamed behind her as she shouldered wizards aside. Finally, she dived into a side passage. Tom almost slammed into her as she stopped before a door. Elenna ducked around the corner, and stopped, breathing hard. Petra thrust the door open.

"Got you!" a woman shouted, as Elenna gave a yelp.

Tom turned to see the red-haired woman clasping his friend's arm. Elenna stamped hard on the woman's foot then leapt through the door after

Petra. Tom followed, slamming the door and throwing his back against it. He stood for a moment, panting, taking in the cosy clutter of Daltec's rooms as the echo of bells faded from his ears. The door behind him shuddered, as if fists were beating at the other side. Daltec strode across the room, waving his hands in a fluid gesture. Tom felt the wooden door at his back shift and grow oddly cold. He turned to find himself looking at grey stone. The door was gone.

"I see you were successful," Daltec said, nodding towards the staff in Tom's hand.

"Only just," Elenna said, rubbing her arm where the woman had clutched her. "They nearly caught us."

"It is well you managed to take the staff," Daltec said. "All over Avantia, thieves from the sky are stealing any metal they can find. Soon there will be no way to shoe our horses or farm the land – let alone defend the City."

Tom gripped the staff in his hand tightly. "It's time to find out what's going on in Henkrall, and put a stop to it once and for all."

Tom gazed out over the stone battlements into the starry night. Beyond the sloping roofs and winding ramparts of the palace, the scattered lights of the City spread out like a dusky map, giving way to the deeper darkness of the surrounding fields.

He turned away from the view to see Alun, the young boy from Henkrall, shivering in his light tunic, his folded wings trembling. Elenna waited beside the boy, while Petra stood apart, her dark hair blowing free and her eyes shining.

"You said you'd take me home," Alun said.

"And I will," Tom answered. He lifted the Lightning Staff into the wind, feeling his stomach clench with excitement and fear. He knew they were about to use an ancient magic so dangerous it was forbidden to even the most powerful sorcerers. Petra stepped forwards and unrolled a sheet of parchment that Daltec had given her.

The witch started to read strange

words. Almost at once, Tom felt a sudden gust of wind whip and whistle around the battlements. He looked up to see dark fingers of cloud quickly clawing their way across the sky, covering the moon and throwing the fields of Avantia into deep shadow. The cloud thickened as it rolled towards them, billowing upwards to form huge, flat-topped thunderheads. The wind tugged at Tom's body and at the staff in his hand.

Petra read on, chanting the peculiar words. Tom felt a prickling energy flow into his body from the Lightning Staff. Petra's guttural voice rose in volume and pitch to carry over the buffeting wind, until she cried, "Henkrall!" Thunder rumbled in the distance and a flash of lightning lit the ramparts below. Petra ran her eyes over the wild, tumultuous sky; then she bowed low, like an actor leaving the stage.

"My work here is done," she said. "Good luck!" She scampered away down the staircase from the tower, leaving them to the gathering storm.

Tom felt the staff give a jolt, sending a shock of energy through him that made every muscle in his body tense. "It's coming!" he shouted, his words snatched by the wind.

Elenna took hold of Tom's elbow. Alun grabbed Tom's other arm.

Lightning forked across the sky. *Crack!* Tom felt a terrible burning pain in his hand as the Lighting

Staff blazed white, blinding him. His muscles cramped and fizzed and his nerves burned as if aflame. For a long, agonising moment everything was white-hot searing pain.

Then the pain was gone. Elenna

and Alun let go of his arms. Tom staggered and almost fell. He blinked to find himself in dull, grey daylight, surrounded by jagged mountains, so high that their tips were lost in cloud. A winding path led past his feet and up the nearest peak to a cluster of wooden huts clinging to the grey rock far above.

"I'm home!" Alun cried.

Elenna stared about at the bleak landscape. "I never thought I'd see Henkrall again," she said.

Alun hurried to the path and started to climb, his wings flapping as he hopped from rock to rock. Tom and Elenna followed behind, scrambling up the steep and winding track.

Tom quickly worked up a fierce

sweat despite the cool breeze and clinging tendrils of mist. It was hard to catch a full breath in the thin mountain air. He shook his head to clear the dizziness. Elenna stumbled, and Tom took her arm. Together they staggered on after the boy. Even before they reached the ramshackle settlement above, Tom could tell that there was something wrong. The only winged form on the mountain seemed to be Alun. There were no goats or goatherds, no farmers or traders – not even a bird. The village itself seemed deserted. The buildings had boarded windows and broken roofs. Pots and clothing lay discarded in the street, and the cooking fires had long ago burned to piles of cold, grey ash.

Alun turned to Tom and Elenna, his wings hanging limp at his sides. He shook his head sadly. "They've taken everyone," he said. "The children. The elderly. Even the sick…" He trailed off, staring at the desolate village.

"But where?" Elenna asked.

Alun swallowed. "I'll show you." The boy dragged his feet now as he led them onwards, his wings folded and his eyes downcast. They followed a narrow, crooked path until it suddenly fell away over a sheer cliff face ahead. Tom could hear the *thud* and *chink* of metal tools echoing up from below.

He crossed to the cliff's edge to look down, and gasped. Hundreds of people in filthy tunics crowded close

together on rickety wooden platforms
built up against the mountainside.
Men, women and children worked
side by side, hacking at the rock face.

All were sunburned red and painfully thin. Worst of all, their white wings were folded and bound together with rope. Only one man flew between the platforms, his wings free and a leather whip in one hand, which he lashed at an old man's leg, leaving a red welt. Fury burned inside Tom's chest.

"They're slaves!" Elenna said. Alun nodded sorrowfully.

Tom balled his fists and waited for his rage to pass. "Whoever is responsible for this," he vowed, "I'll make them pay."

6

A CROOKED PLAN

Suddenly Alun grabbed Tom's arm and pointed. "Mother!" he cried.

"Shhh!" Tom clamped a hand over Alun's mouth as a tall woman glanced up towards them. Rock dust covered her tanned skin, and her back was stooped beneath a huge basket loaded with rock.

As her gaze fell on Alun, she gave a relieved smile, but then her eyes opened wide with alarm.

At the same moment, a shadow fell over Tom from above.

"Tom!" Elenna cried.

Tom turned to see four huge, winged men swooping down from the sky, nets slung between them. They dropped one over Elenna, scooping her into the air. Another net whistled towards Tom. He swiped at the ropes with his sword, but the blade tangled in the twine. The net closed about him and his stomach lurched as his attackers climbed sharply, hoisting him skywards. The mine fell away below. From the air, Tom could see the full, sickening scale of it. It seemed like every citizen of Henkrall was toiling down there.

Before long, a veil of mist and cloud

blanked the view. Still they climbed, up through the freezing cloud and out again into clear blue sky. Snow-capped mountain peaks jutted up around them. Tom could see Elenna ahead, her elbows and knees pressed tight to the mesh of her net. Tom

noticed that her captors each carried a dagger and a sword, as well as crossbows slung across their backs. From their weather-worn leathers and mismatched weapons, he guessed they were mercenaries.

Tom's jaw tightened as he spotted a familiar mountain peak ahead, climbing far above the rest. Jutting from the mountain's craggy face were the slate-topped towers of Kensa's former castle. The Evil Witch had deserted it during Tom's last Quest in Henkrall, but he noticed an ominous red glow coming from the narrow windows of its main hall. *Has Kensa returned?* he wondered.

The mercenaries swooped towards an open platform of stone built out from the main entrance of the hall. Tom felt the net go slack around him. His heart skipped as he started to fall, just before hard grey stone slammed into his side, punching the breath from his body. Elenna tumbled to the ground beside him, rolled, then scrambled from her net. Tom glanced back to see their four captors glowering at him from behind hefty crossbows.

"We have caught the trespassers!" one of the mercenaries shouted.

Tom turned in time to see the castle doors creak open. He braced himself to face his old enemy once again...

But it wasn't Kensa who emerged from the castle. Instead, a hunched figure with straggly hair scraped thinly across his mottled scalp shuffled forwards. The man's single bloodshot eye glittered as it fell on Tom.

Igor!

Kensa's old servant looked more haggard than ever, the grisly stumps on his shoulders a stark reminder of where Kensa had removed his wings. Igor's lips spread into a strange, lopsided grimace. It took a moment for Tom to realise he was smiling.

"Kneel before our leader!" snarled one of the mercenaries.

Tom took a step towards Igor, his fists balled. "What have you done?" he cried. "Oof!" A heavy kick landed in the small of Tom's back, sending him sprawling. He tried to stand,

but big hands clamped down on his
shoulders, forcing him to his knees.

"Be still!" the man holding Tom
snapped. Tom felt the sharp prickle
of a knife between his shoulder-

blades. He stopped struggling, seething with fury.

"That's better!" Igor said. "Strip the prisoners of their weapons!"

Tom's shield was wrenched from his back and his sword tugged from its sheath. Rough hands dug into his arms and he was jerked to his feet.

"Follow me!" said Igor.

The hunchback turned and hobbled through the palace doors. Tom and Elenna were shoved after him, into a vast circular hall carved out of the mountain, filled with a smouldering red light. The heat in the room stung Tom's skin. Wooden shelves crowded with books, glass bottles and phials ran around the curved walls. A workbench stood nearby, cluttered with a jumble of clay moulds and dog-eared spell books. The flickering light and infernal heat came from six blazing fires set in stone hearths built around a huge central pit. Men and women with bound wings worked bellows and tossed stolen metal artefacts into crucibles set over the roaring flames.

Other workers poured molten metal into long channels cut into the stone floor. Glowing rivulets of liquid metal ran in blues and oranges and burning golds towards the black pit at the centre of the room – the dead heart of an ancient volcano.

"Since Kensa left me here in charge, I have been experimenting with her magic," Igor said. "She will be proud of what I have achieved."

Tom turned away, trying to make out the purpose of the noisy workshop. Rough-looking mercenaries armed with crossbows and swords moved between the

workers. Ropes and pulleys ran across the ceiling, leading to the pit in the stone floor. A woman in a ragged tunic rummaged through a pile of glinting metal and tossed a delicate gold crown into a pot over one of the fires.

"That belongs to Queen Aroha!" Tom cried.

Igor nodded. "Mixing the metals together makes them stronger," he said. "I had to scour every kingdom for all the right ingredients, but now I have all the metal I need."

"For what?" Tom asked, anger and dread churning inside him. Igor had amassed enough metal to arm every man, woman and child in Henkrall.

"Take a look," Igor said, pointing towards the pit.

Tom stepped forwards with Elenna at his side, the heavy feeling inside him building. Together they peered into the pit.

Elenna gasped. "What is that thing?"

A huge clay figure, roughly the shape

of a man but taller than a house, stood in the centre of the pit. It reminded Tom of the clay figures Kensa had once used to create Beasts – but this was far bigger, and lacked the detail of Kensa's models. Molten metal poured from the grooves scored in the rock floor, down long clay spouts suspended from ropes, and into an opening at the top of the clay shape.

It's not a model – it's a cast, Tom realised. *But for what?* He turned to Igor.

"You're making a statue?" Tom asked, with a puzzled frown.

The hunchback grinned back at him. "Not a statue," Igor said. "I'm making my very own Beast. You've come just in time to see it wake!"

THE BIRTH OF A MONSTER

Tom stared at Igor's twitching face, lit up horribly by the glow from the fires. His single round eye seemed to bulge with pride.

"You've gone mad," Tom said. "Why would you want to create a Beast?"

Igor spread his hands. "To do my bidding, of course," he said.

"What makes you think it will do

as you say?" Elenna asked. "You're no Master of the Beasts."

Igor shot her a look of pure hatred, then hobbled to a huge lever set in the ground. His twisted shoulders strained as he wrenched at the wooden handle. Tom heard a *whirr* and a *clunk*, then all the clay spouts feeding molten metal into the clay cast lifted, cutting off the supply.

"All I need now is one final ingredient," Igor said. "The blood of a Master of the Beasts!" He lifted a hand. "Men!"

Two greasy-haired thugs lurched from the shadows and flapped towards Tom.

"I don't think so," Tom said, lifting his fists ready to fight.

"Tom!" Elenna cried.

Tom glanced back to see three broad men aiming crossbows at her chest. The fight went out of him in an instant. He let his fists fall. One of the mercenaries grabbed his shoulders while the other snatched hold of his wrist and tugged back the sleeve.

Igor sidled up to Tom, stopping so close Tom could smell the mustiness of his grimy clothes and greasy hair. The hunchback's single eye glinted hungrily as he leered at Tom. Then he pulled a rusty blade from a pouch at his belt. Tom flinched as Igor rested the cold edge against his wrist.

Igor chuckled. "Don't move," he said, "or I might end up taking more blood than I intend. And I have no

wish to kill you. Yet…"

Tom gritted his teeth and held as
still as he could while Igor drew the
blade across his skin. Blood welled
from a shallow cut. Igor scrabbled in
his pouch, drewing out a phial. He
held the lip of the phial to Tom's wrist,

letting dark drops collect inside.

"That should be enough," Igor said.

Tom felt the mercenaries release him. He drew back his arm, pressing his hand to the cut. The two big men stepped to either side of Igor, gripped him under the arms and rose into the air, carrying the wingless hunchback with them, over the pit to the opening at the head of the clay cast. Igor upturned his phial and let Tom's blood trickle into the mould.

The mercenaries set Igor back on his feet near the edge of the pit. He lifted his hands.

"Arise, my metal warrior!" he cried.

At first, nothing seemed to happen. But then Tom heard a muffled *crack*, followed by more *crackles* and *pings*.

The ground beneath Tom's feet gave a shudder, and then – *BOOM!* – the cast exploded.

Tom threw up his arms to shield his face as chunks of clay hurtled towards him. A huge block struck his chest, knocking him backwards. Smaller fragments pattered down on his head and shoulders. Cries of panic rang out from the workers in the room. Choking dust filled the air, glowing like angry red smoke in the light from the fires. When the air cleared, Tom saw Igor crouched, staring into the pit. He moved to the hunchback's side, and his guts twisted with terror. In the centre of the pit, a gleaming metal giant turned slowly, surveying the wreckage.

As the huge metal head swivelled to face Igor, a shiver ran down Tom's spine. Where the Beast's eyes should have been, dark hollows gaped, as cold and empty as open graves. The Beast's square features shone in the fiery light, but his expression was as blank as a corpse.

"Do you hear me, slave?" Igor cried. "I created you! You must do as I say!"

Tom heard the Beast's reply in his mind, his voice a rasping roar like the hiss of sparks hitting water. *I hear you, puny creature. But I am no slave. I am Kyrax!*

The Beast tipped his vast head from side to side and flexed his giant shoulders.

"Stop!" Igor cried. A huge metal

hand gripped the side of the pit, then another. The Beast started to heave himself up. Tom heard the sound of wingbeats and glanced back to see Igor's mercenaries flapping through the door. Free of their guards, the workers scrambled to untie each other's wings, then soared after their captors.

"Obey me!" Igor screamed, spit flying from his lips and his one eye bulging. The Beast's head emerged from the pit, then his torso. Already he towered above them.

Tom put his hand to the red jewel in his belt. *I am Master of the Beasts*, he told the giant. *My blood gave you life, Kyrax. I order you to stop!*

The Beast ignored him, his hollow eyes fixed on Igor as he clambered

from the pit. Tom staggered back,
but Igor didn't move. Instead, the
hunchback cowered, seemingly frozen
with fear as Kyrax reached out and
gripped the back of his tunic between
two vast fingers. The giant lifted the
hunchback until the two were face to
face, and stared hard into Igor's wide,
terrified eye. A faint curl of disgust
stirred the Beast's metallic features
as, with a flick of his massive wrist,
he tossed Igor across the room like
a piece of rubbish, out through the
chamber doors and down the side of
the mountain. Igor let out a hideous
screech of terror, then fell silent.

"Find a weapon, quick!" Tom called
to Elenna. He raced towards a pile of
metal and tugged a spear free.

Kyrax's colossal head turned slowly, until his dark eye sockets fell on Tom. The Beast started to move, taking long, steady strides. Terror squeezed Tom's chest. He drew back his arm and let the spear fly.

It struck Kyrax's broad chest and sank deep. The metal surrounding the wound shimmered, and a spark of kindled briefly in the Beast's hollow eyes. Suddenly, the wooden spear shaft shot from the Beast's body, straight back towards Tom. He leapt aside, and it clattered to the ground, now missing its metal tip. When Tom looked up at the Beast, he saw no mark where the spear had struck.

"Tom! I've found our weapons!" Elenna called, grabbing her bow from the ground.

"Wait!" Tom cried, but she let an arrow fly. It struck Kyrax's leg. The Beast's eyes flashed once more as they turned on Elenna.

Whoosh! The arrow shaft sliced back towards her, its metal head gone. Elenna swung her bow and knocked the wooden missile aside.

The terrible sizzling hiss of the Beast's voice filled Tom's mind. *Your weapons only make me stronger!*

Tom raced to Elenna's side and snatched up his sword and shield.

"He can absorb metal!" Elenna said.

Tom nodded. He shoved his sword into its scabbard, his mind racing. Kyrax started towards them, his empty eyes fixed on Elenna.

He's going to kill her!

Tom lifted his shield, called on the magic of his golden breastplate, ducked his head, and charged.

The Beast's fist shot out and closed about Tom's body, snatching him up like a toy. Tom struggled, but even using all his magical strength, he couldn't twist free.

"Let him go!" Elenna shouted, beating her fists against Kyrax's metal flesh. But the Beast's fingers tightened steadily around him.

Tom closed his eyes, terror pounding through him with every heartbeat, bracing himself for the agony of being crushed. But instead, he felt a cold numbness seeping into his body where the giant's fingers touched his flesh. Even his blood seemed to cool in his veins.

Now the power you yield shall be mine! roared the Beast.

Tom opened his eyes to see Kyrax's huge chest covered by a giant-sized version of his golden breastplate. He glanced up to see the Beast's empty eye sockets staring down at him from a vast copy of his golden helmet. The armour shimmered before his eyes. Swirling silver lines appeared across its golden surface, then it vanished, absorbed into the giant's metal flesh.

Tom's stomach roiled with dread. *This Beast is so powerful, he can summon the Golden Armour to him, even from a kingdom away!*

Thank you, said Kyrax, relaxing the

metal fingers that held Tom.

Thud! Tom hit the ground like a bundle of rags and lay there, gasping, bruised and shivering. An emptiness welled inside him.

The power of his Golden Armour was gone.

STORY TWO

A BATTLE OF THE BEASTS

Sometimes, Tom and Elenna are just too brave for their own good. I know I said I wanted some adventure, but taking the Lightning Path to Henkrall, of all places, is madness!

There's nothing for them in Henkrall but savage winged people, and a crazy, one-eyed hunchback who still wants revenge for his Evil mistress. Now, Igor has created a terrible Beast that will wreak havoc on Avantia if it manages to get here.

Tom and Elenna will stop it. They have to. Otherwise, Avantia could be doomed.

Maybe I should have gone with them...

Petra the witch

WARRIOR OF THE SKIES

Elenna fell to Tom's side and tugged at his arm. Tom staggered towards the door on shaking legs. He felt weak, but fury drove him on.

I earned that armour and Kyrax stole it! He glanced back to see the Beast gaining on them with colossal strides. Elenna scooped up a huge lump of broken clay mould and hurled it. The fragile clay shattered against the giant's metal temple.

But Kyrax just shook his head and marched on over the debris.

"Get behind there!" Elenna cried, pointing to a cauldron of molten metal bubbling over a fire. Tom dived behind the stone hearth and squatted low. Elenna raced to his side.

"What now?" Tom asked as the thud of metal footsteps drew closer. Elenna grabbed a pair of leather gloves from the ground, leapt to her feet and shoved the crucible over. Tom peered from behind the hearth to see liquid metal splash across the floor and splatter against the leg of Igor's workbench. Kyrax leapt back with a hiss of fury. The wood fizzled and hissed. Flames licked up the table leg, catching the edge of a book. A phial of something on the bench exploded, sending out a shower of glass and more flames.

Kyrax lifted the burning table with a furious roar and flung it from him across the room. It smashed into another hearth, toppling the crucible that was perched there. Fiery metal spattered across the floor towards wooden shelving crowded with books. Choking smoke quickly filled the chamber. The Beast started to back away from the spreading flames, towards the door. As Kyrax turned and stepped into daylight, Tom saw the Beast's shoulders bulge outwards then spread, thinning and branching, forming hundreds of gleaming feathers.

Tom watched in horror as the Beast
flexed a pair of immense, metal wings.

*He's a giant made of metal...our
weapons only make him stronger –
and now he can fly!*

The Beast flapped, once, twice, then
tipped off the stone platform and
soared out over the mountains.

Tom and Elenna sprang up. The whole chamber seemed ablaze. Flames raged along the wooden bookshelves, licking towards the ceiling. Thick black smoke filled the air, stinging Tom's eyes and throat. He and Elenna ran for the door. Smoke billowed around them as they raced out on to the high, open entrance platform jutting from the mountainside. The setting sun cast smouldering rays on to the heavy storm clouds gathering above. The Beast gleamed in the darkening sky, reflecting the fiery light like a giant phoenix as he soared away.

"We have to go after him," Elenna said, shielding her eyes against the wind. "But how?"

"I have no idea," Tom said.

"Help me!" A weedy cry came from below them, almost snatched away on the strengthening gale.

Tom peered over the edge of the platform and spotted a narrow shelf of rock not far below where they stood. Huddled on the shelf, clinging to the rock face for dear life, was Igor.

"Maybe he'll know how to defeat the Beast," Tom said. "Kyrax is his creation, after all. Wait here."

Tom covered his mouth and nose with his sleeve, then ducked back into the blazing workshop. He soon spotted what he needed – a length of rope, probably left over from Igor's pulley system. Keeping low to the ground, he crossed the chamber, grabbed the rope, then dashed for the door.

By the time Tom and Elenna had pulled the grey-faced hunchback up on to the platform, huge, heavy drops of rain had started to fall.

"Thank you!" Igor said. He pawed at Tom's tunic with his knobbly

fingers. "I've made a terrible mistake. I didn't realise my mistress's magic could cause such harm!"

Tom's skin crawled with disgust. "Don't try to pretend you didn't know full well what you were doing. Tell us – how do we defeat this Beast?"

The hunchback winced, cringing even lower than before. "Kyrax was designed to be invincible," he said.

Tom shook his head, frustration building inside him. "He must have a weak spot. Every Beast does."

Igor gave a flinching, lopsided shrug. "Metal weapons just make him stronger, and you won't get close enough to hurt him. Our best option is to flee Henkrall."

Tom could hardly believe what he

was hearing. "We're going nowhere," he said. "My blood and your greed created Kyrax. Whatever the danger, whatever the cost, we're going to defeat that monster!"

2

A DEADLY PLAY FOR TIME

Rain pelted against Tom's tunic and plastered his hair to his scalp as the last rays of weak sunlight faded from the tattered sky, which was split by a streak of lightning. Above the rumble of thunder, Tom heard the terrified neigh of a horse, followed by the bloodcurdling squeal of a pig.

He turned to Igor. "Are there animals

trapped inside the castle?" Tom asked.

Igor shrugged. "Just the dumb ones in the stable tower. We should leave them and escape while we can."

"I won't abandon innocent creatures to die," Tom said. "Show me the way."

Igor scowled, but turned and led Tom and Elenna into the smoke-filled chamber. They came to a narrow alcove that led to a spiral staircase. Through the smothering gloom, Tom could hear the sound of the panicked animals.

Elenna pushed past Igor, taking the stairs two at a time. Tom raced to her side, wishing he had the power of his golden boots. His eyes burned, his chest rasped and he felt dizzy with the fumes as he climbed. They burst into a stable. They could barely see for the smoke, but Tom could pick out the animals huddled against the far side of the room – two tall winged horses and Igor's flying hog, along with a few hens and a winged cow and calf. Riding tack hung on the wall. Tom and Elenna raced to the horses, offering comforting strokes and soft words while preparing them to ride. Igor arrived just as Tom swung into his saddle. The hunchback's winged hog greeted him with an ear-splitting squeal.

"All right, all right," Igor grunted, climbing on to the creature's back. "I'll save your life, if I have to!"

Tom rode to the stable doors,

unhooked the wooden latch and thrust them open. A fierce wind caught the doors, banging them against the tower wall which fell away to meet sharp rocks far below. The wind whipped at Tom, filling his lungs with clean air. Smoke billowed past out into the storm. A silvery streak of lightning cracked from above, briefly outlining the rocky landscape of Henkrall. A moment later, thunder boomed and grumbled around them. Tom gripped his horse's reins firmly and pressed his heels to the creature's sides.

I hope you're as steady as you seem, Tom thought. *It's a long way down...*

The stallion unfurled its wings and beat them hard, leaping out into

the storm. Tom glanced back to see
Elenna and Igor following. The other
animals poured from the stable,
scattering into the night.

Tom narrowed his eyes into the wind, looking for any sign of Kyrax. Elenna flew at his side, with Igor just behind. Wild gusts buffeted against them but their mounts flew straight and true. Suddenly, the whole sky lit up with a flash of lightning. Thunder cracked overhead. Tom saw in the flare of brightness a vast figure, riding the storm on wide, shining wings.

Kyrax!

As Tom watched, the Beast balled a fist and raised it high. Another bolt of lightning crackled down. The Beast seemed to snatch it from the sky then cast it from him in a ball of searing white energy. The ball of light flared and widened, becoming a jagged tear in the sky. Through the opening, Tom could see daylight, and endless fields of swaying grass. *Avantia!*

His heart plummeted as he saw the Beast pass through the portal, flying out over Avantia's Central Plains. The portal began to dwindle at once.

"We must reach the portal before it closes!" Tom cried.

"Not I!" Igor shouted, tugging the reins of his hog.

"Oh no, you don't!" Elenna cried. Before the hog could turn, Elenna leaned from her saddle, grabbed Igor under the arms and hauled him on to her horse. "You started this and you'll see it through," she said. Then she dug her heels into her horse's sides and raced towards the portal.

Tom leaned low over his stallion's

neck, willing it towards the narrowing tear in the sky. The horse's wings beat fast and hard, pounding at the air. Just as it seemed there was barely room to fit through, the stallion reached the portal and soared into the daylight. Tom suddenly found himself flying high over lush green prairie.

Ahead, Kyrax banked steeply down towards the rippling grass. He landed in a run and furled his mighty wings, then turned to survey the terrain. Tom glanced back to see Elenna and Igor flapping towards him. The portal was gone.

"Go to the City and warn the king to prepare for battle!" Tom called to Elenna. "I'll keep the Beast busy to give you time."

"But how will you fight it?" Elenna asked.

Tom swallowed. "I'll think of something," he said. *I'll have to...* Then he urged his horse towards the metal giant. While Elenna swerved towards the distant city, Tom lifted his shield and readied himself for the hardest battle he'd ever faced. He couldn't use his sword. He had no armour. All he had was his wits.

As Tom directed his winged horse towards Kyrax, the Beast turned. Kyrax lifted a vast fist and swatted at the stallion. Tom tugged at the horse's reins, forcing the terrified animal to swerve away from the Beast's metal fist, bringing it down to land. As soon as the horse's hooves touched the ground, Tom swung from the saddle. The stallion opened its wings, leapt back into the air and swooped skyward.

"Leave this place!" Tom called up to Kyrax. "Return to Henkrall. You have no business here."

The Beast tipped back its head and let out a long roar of crackling laughter. *Never!* he cried. Then he lifted an arm. The metal shimmered like quicksilver and ran together, lengthening and narrowing. In a heartbeat, the arm had reformed in the shape of a giant sword. Tom's hand fell to the hilt of his own sword, but he left it sheathed.

I can't use metal... And he knew his shield would never withstand a blow from such a weapon.

Kyrax stabbed downwards. Tom leapt aside, his heart thundering, just managing to dodge the blow as it raked a groove in the ground. The

Beast's empty eye sockets gazed down at Tom. It lifted the colossal weapon once more.

Swoosh! The giant blade swiped sideways in a wide arc headed straight for Tom's chest. Tom darted back, and the blade flashed past, its wicked point slicing the air. Tom circled, his mouth dry and his body prickling with cold sweat.

I have to give Elenna time.

The Beast lunged and jabbed. Tom leapt and ducked. He focussed his mind on the glinting blade, diving and rolling from its path. But each time he escaped a lethal swipe, another came, faster and closer. Tom's movements began to slow. His breathing was ragged and his legs felt as heavy as lead. As he sprang away from a fierce strike, his boot snagged on a tuft of grass. He landed hard, flat on his back. The Beast let his blade arm fall and strode to Tom's side. Empty eye sockets gazed down at Tom as he raised one giant foot. Tom watched, helpless, as the vast metal sole hovered above him.

Your days end now, feeble boy, Kyrax told Tom in a crackling roar inside his head. *I will crush your bones to dust!*

3

BATTLE OF THE PLAIN

The ground trembled and Kyrax turned. The sound of hoofbeats thundered in Tom's ears. *A horse?*

A blur rushed past. *No! Not a horse. A Beast!*

"Tagus!" Tom cried.

CLANG! The horse-man's mighty blade slashed through the metal of Kyrax's supporting ankle, almost

severing the foot. Kyrax roared as his damaged leg buckled. Tom rolled, throwing himself out of the shadow of the falling fiend. A colossal thud rocked the ground.

So a Beast's blade can harm Kyrax, Tom thought, as he scrambled away on trembling legs. He glanced back and saw Kyrax heave himself up to standing. As he watched, the metal of the Beast's injured foot shimmered and flowed to fill the gash made by Tagus's sword. The Good Beast's eyes blazed with fury as he glared up at the metal warrior, but Kyrax stood three times his height and more than twice as broad.

Bravely, Tagus raked the earth with his hoof, ducked his head and charged. Kyrax stepped aside and snapped out his bladed arm.

SMASH! Tom winced as Kyrax smashed the horse-man's sword aside, then slashed him across the flank. Tagus let out a bellow of pain. His front legs buckled and he slumped to the ground, snorting for breath, blood welling from his side.

Kyrax stood over his fallen opponent, lifted his sword and shook it. The metal warrior's body shone gold in the sun, dazzling to look at, but the gaping hollows of his eyes were filled with shadows as dark as the tomb.

Now I will suck this new land dry! Kyrax declared, lowering his bladed arm, opening his wings and rising into the sky, before flying south towards the City.

Tom leapt up and raced to Tagus's side. The Good Beast gingerly rose to all fours.

Are you all right? Tom asked, using the power of his red jewel.

Tagus shook his tangled main of hair back and let out a snort. *It is nothing more than a scratch*, he told Tom. *It will mend.*

Tom nodded. *Thank you, brave friend. I owe you my life.* Tagus let out a whinny, then cantered away across the plains.

Tom lifted his eyes to the southern horizon. Kyrax was already out of sight, but a dark silhouette circling above the plains caught Tom's eye.

My horse! He put his fingers to his lips and let out a piercing whistle. To Tom's relief, the Henkrall stallion let out an answering neigh, banking and landing neatly on the ground. Tom swung up into the saddle and kicked the horse's sides. The stallion beat its wings, and Tom felt speed tug at his stomach as they climbed. He bent into the wind, riding hard and fast towards the City.

Grassland rolled past below him, then snaking streams and a patchwork of farms. Eventually the flat countryside gave way to gentle hills and scattered villages lying peacefully in the morning sun. In the distance, Tom could see the towers and spires of the City.

As Tom drew nearer, he saw
billowing clouds of dust rising up
from the road that led to the city
gates. He heard distant shouts and
metallic clangs on the wind; he saw
the armour of hundreds of soldiers
glinting in the sun as mounted
troops and foot soldiers poured
out from the City, spreading across
the field. *Harkman's army!* Tom
realised, speeding onwards. Soon
he could make out banners, horses
and catapults firing flaming barrels.
The vast, gleaming form of the Beast
towered over the mounted men and
foot soldiers, moving this way and
that, advancing, then drawing back to
avoid the flaming projectiles. Seeing
the metal warrior dodge the fiery

artillery, Tom remembered how Kyrax had fled the fire in Kensa's castle.

Flames melt metal… Tom thought, an idea growing. He put his hand to Ferno's scale, embedded in his shield. He felt the scale grow warm.

Come quickly to the City! Tom told the Good Beast, hoping he was close enough to help. *We are under attack!*

The flying horse's flanks heaved as Tom pushed him harder and faster towards the battle raging outside the city walls. Hope kindled inside Tom as a fiery barrel caught Kyrax square on the cheek, sending him spinning, flames engulfing his head.

When they died away, Tom saw one side of the Beast's face had melted into a smeared and blackened mess.

Kyrax staggered, his foot catching on a boulder, and then fell down with a mighty crash.

A roar of triumph went up from Harkman's army. They surged towards the fallen Beast, swarming over it and fastening chains about its arms and legs.

Metal chains...

"No!" Tom cried. "Use ropes, not chains!" He urged the horse on, but there was no way he could reach the soldiers in time. The fallen giant shook his head angrily and the chains that covered its body shimmered and melted away, becoming part of the Beast. Harkman's men let out shouts of alarm and started to flee as the Beast pulled himself up, sending the

remaining men scattering. Kyrax
towered over the soldiers as they ran,
then lifted his head and let out a roar

of fury. He raised one mighty foot and stamped, shattering a catapult to smithereens. A powerful kick sent another scaffold flying. Horses reared and screamed, bucking their riders, and men ran for their lives.

Tom saw Harkman lift a horn. A deep note boomed across the field. "Retreat!" Tom heard Harkman cry. His words were echoed by his men, who were fleeing towards the City. Tom watched the chaos with growing dread as he sped towards the Beast.

If an army couldn't defeat Kyrax, what hope did a lone boy without a weapon have?

4

A SHARD OF HOPE

Before Tom could reach Kyrax, the metal giant spread his wings and leapt into the air, heading straight for the city walls. Tom's heart clenched at the thought of all the innocent people inside.

I can't let Kyrax harm them! Tom heard the swish of wings behind him. He glanced over his shoulder, feeling a thrill of hope when he saw the vast, shape of Ferno soaring towards him.

Tom raised a hand in greeting.
Ferno let out a puff of smoke, then
banked, swooping low beside Tom's
horse. Tom gave his horse a parting
stroke. "I'll be back for you!" he told

the animal. Then he sized up the gap, took a deep breath, and leapt from the saddle. He whistled through the air and landed on the dragon's back. He straddled the Good Beast's neck and leaned into the wind.

Ferno let out a low growl. *That Beast should not exist*, he said, speaking through Tom's red jewel.

"Fire gave birth to it, and fire is its enemy," Tom replied.

Then fire it shall get!

The city walls loomed ahead of them – all that protected Avantia's capital from Kyrax's wrath. Ferno surged forwards with a sudden burst of speed that snatched Tom's breath away. As they drew up behind the metal warrior, the dragon's huge jaws opened to blast a searing stream of flame which engulfed Kyrax's massive wings. The Evil Beast let out a hideous roar. Tom saw Kyrax's wings blacken and fold, melting away. When Ferno's fiery breath was spent, only twisted stumps remained. Kyrax flapped his gnarled wings frantically, but could not keep himself airborne. With a hiss of fury, he plummeted towards the earth.

Crash! The city walls rocked and stones tumbled down as Kyrax landed just outside the gates. The Beast staggered to his feet, flexing its metal wings as they reformed before Tom's eyes. Tom guided Ferno down towards the ground, and the dragon let out another jet of flame. Tom saw the

stern lines of Kyrax's face soften and blur in the heat. Ferno turned sharply, looping away from the Evil Beast to come in for another attack. Kyrax's colossal sword-arm sliced upwards as the dragon swept past. Ferno let out a bellow of pain, and Tom saw dark blood spatter the ground, dripping from a gash in the dragon's underbelly. Ferno's wingbeats faltered and he careened towards the field. Tom clung tight to the Good Beast's scales as the ground sped up to meet them.

Ferno's legs buckled and his chest ploughed through the earth. Tom lost his grip and flew over the dragon's head. He tucked himself into a roll as he landed, then sprang up. Ferno lurched unsteadily to his feet, staggering around to face Kyrax again. The metal warrior stood tall before the city gate, his wings re-formed and his features sharp once more.

You cannot destroy me! The Beast's voice was scratchy and

metallic inside Tom's head.

"Tom!" It was Elenna. Tom looked up to see her flying her winged horse just above the city walls. "Igor says Kyrax may have a weak spot," she called. "At his heart, there is a small clay figure. If you can destroy that, you will destroy the Beast."

Of course, Tom thought, remembering how Kensa had constructed new Beasts from clay figurines. *The hunchback is using the witch's methods. He could have told us that earlier!*

But the memory gave him little hope. The vast metal monster before him was taller and more powerful than any Beast Tom had faced.

Kyrax lunged towards him,

swinging his huge blade downwards in a blow that could cleave Tom in half. Tom leapt back out of reach. The blade crashed down, biting deep into the earth. Kyrax tugged, trying to free his arm, but it didn't budge.

He's stuck!

Ferno gave a roar of triumph. He extended his long neck towards Kyrax, opened his mouth and breathed out flickering tongues of fire. The flames engulfed Kyrax's sword arm. The Beast's furious face shimmered in a heat haze from the blast consuming his limb. Suddenly, Kyrax was free. He staggered back, his sword half the length it had been, ending in a blackened stump. Tom saw a small crater in the ground. At its base, a pool of shiny molten metal cooled and hardened.

The weapon of a Beast… Tom remembered Tagus's sword slicing Kyrax's foot. *If I had a blade like that I might stand a chance!*

While Kyrax stared at his severed arm, Tom leapt forwards and prised

the smoking lump of metal up with
the tip of his sword. The sleeve of his
tunic, torn from his fall, hung loose
at his shoulder. He yanked it hard,
ripping it off, then used it to lift
the disc of metal. Even through the
folded fabric, he could feel the heat
burning his hand.

"Elenna!" he called. "Take this to
Henry. Tell him I need him to make a
sword from it – and fast!"

Elenna's steed dived from the
battlements and glided towards
him. Tom lifted the disc of scorching
metal, and Elenna leaned from her
saddle and snatched it up, gripping
the folded fabric of Tom's sleeve.

Kyrax stamped a metal foot, lifted
his blade arm skywards and let out

a fierce battle cry. The sun flashed against the silvery metal of his sword as it re-formed – narrower than it had been before, but just as sharp.

Kyrax fixed Tom with his dead, dark eyes and Tom heard the Beast's voice in his mind. *Now you die!*

5

FERNO THE BRAVE

As the Beast lunged towards him, Tom heard a growl.

Boof! Ferno's snout ploughed into his side, thrusting him clear of Kyrax's attack.

Kyrax turned, lunging for Tom, but the fire dragon blocked his path with a jet of white-hot flame.

Go and make your sword, Ferno growled in Tom's mind.

Tom sprinted towards the city gates. They flew open and two terrified guards beckoned Tom inside, then slammed and barred the doors.

As Tom ran across the courtyard, he heard the rumbles and roars of two Beasts going to battle outside the walls. He saw smoke billowing from the forge. He dived into the half-darkness to find Henry shovelling fuel on to a roaring fire. Elenna stood at his side, working the bellows, her face shiny and her short hair standing up. Harkman paced the room, his fists balled. Igor cringed in a corner, flanked by two guards.

Henry glanced at Tom. "I need to get the forge hotter," he said. "This metal is like none I've ever worked with."

Tom seized a pair of bellows, crossed to Elenna's side and got to work.

The heat was terrific. Tom's skin soon poured with sweat and his eyes smarted. A soldier came to the door and Harkman crossed to meet him. He turned back to them, his face grim.

"Ferno fights bravely, but he is wounded and weakening," he said. "My men cannot defeat this Beast. If Kyrax breaches the city walls, many will die."

Tom felt a stab of fear for the dragon. "Get the people to the tunnels beneath the palace," he said. "As soon as the sword is ready, I will join Ferno and defeat this Beast."

Harkman nodded, turned on his heel and was gone. Tom heard him barking orders. "Evacuate the City!"

"At last!" Henry cried. Tom looked to see the metal in the crucible losing its form, shimmering at the edges and then melting into a silvery liquid.

"Stand back." Henry took up a pair of tongs, lifted the crucible, and poured the molten metal into a long, slender mould. Steam bubbled from the neck of the cast. As soon as the bubbling stopped, Henry cracked the mould open with a chisel, revealing a bright blade. Henry laid the sword on his anvil and started hammering the glowing metal.

Suddenly, through the clang of Henry's mallet, Tom heard Ferno's voice in his mind – a weak growl, barely more than a breath. *I cannot hold him. The fight needs you, Master.*

Ferno's words spurred Tom to desperate haste. He took a leather rag from a pile, and stepped towards his uncle. "The Beast is in the City," Tom said. "Soon, he will breach the walls of the palace. I need the sword now."

Henry frowned. "It's not ready. It

needs hammering and grinding."

"There's no time!" Tom grabbed the hilt with his rag and plunged the blade into a barrel of water, sending up a plume of fizzing steam.

When Tom drew the sword from the water, he gasped. Swirls of rainbow colours danced across the metal. The blade was ragged-edged but straight, and it tapered to a wicked point.

Henry gave a shaky sigh. "It might do," he said.

Tom turned to Elenna. "Go to the tunnels with Henry," he said. "You will be safe there until the battle is over."

"No!" she said. "I won't leave you."

"Only one can wield this blade," Tom said. "If you're with me, I'll have to protect you. I need you to go."

Elenna bit her lip, holding Tom's gaze. At last, she nodded.

Tom hefted his new weapon, feeling its balance. "I won't let you down," he said. "While there's blood in my veins, the City will not fall!"

6

COURAGE AND SACRIFICE

Bright sunlight and cool air hit Tom as he burst from the forge into the courtyard.

From beyond the palace walls, he heard Ferno roar with pain, just before part of the wall exploded inwards. Ferno's huge body burst through and slid across the cobbles. Lumps of stone rained down.

"Oof!" Tom gasped, as he felt a jolting blow to his temple. His sword went flying, and he sank to his knees as pain filled his senses, his eyes filling with water. He shook his head and blinked hard. The courtyard came back into focus, but then lurched into a sickening spin. Through his whirling vision, Tom saw Ferno slumped on the ground. The brave Beast had deep cuts scored into the scales of his side. His orange eyes were narrow slits and his flanks barely moved with each breath. Tom staggered towards Ferno as the City seemed to tip and spin.

With a battle cry, Kyrax leapt over the broken wall and landed in the courtyard, his feet hitting the cobbles

with a deafening metallic clang. Tom scanned the dust and debris around him for any sign of his blade, then scrabbled in the dirt, blinking to focus his eyes as he hunted for the magical weapon.

No Beast of Avantia is strong

enough to stop me, said Kyrax into Tom's mind. *I will finish the dragon, and then I will finish you, Master of the Beasts!*

Tom's eyes caught a fleeting movement on the battlements above – a soldier, dressed in full armour and wielding what looked like a blacksmith's mallet.

As the metal warrior lifted a giant foot towards Ferno's neck, the soldier made a mighty leap, flying through the air to land right on Kyrax's shoulder. Tom watched in awe as the armoured figure brought his mallet down with a hollow clang. Kyrax spun on one foot and lurched sideways, away from Ferno. The soldier clung to the Beast's

head, striking the wooden mallet at
his temple, again and again. Kyrax
bellowed in rage and staggered
through the debris, the soldier
clinging on for dear life.

Tom saw a glint of metal a few
paces away. He reached down,

clawing rubble aside, and his fingers
closed about the hilt of his sword.
The leather rag to protect his grip
had fallen away, but the blade was
undamaged.

As Tom focussed his swimming
vision on the Evil Beast, he saw
Kyrax draw back his massive hand.
Cold horror surged through Tom as
the Beast swatted the soldier away
from his head like a fly. The armoured
figure flew through the air, slammed
into the courtyard wall, then landed
in a twisted heap with a sickening
crunch.

Tom gritted his teeth, gathered
together all his strength and fixed his
gaze on Kyrax's broad, shining chest.
A burning energy flooded through

his veins, fuelled by fury, sorrow and guilt. Tom threw himself forwards, leaping over fallen blocks of stone, charging full speed towards the Beast. Kyrax turned towards Tom, drawing back his colossal blade arm. Tom ran on, the fallen form of the brave soldier in his mind. As he neared the Beast, he bent his knees and leapt as if he still had the power of his golden boots. He sprang up, over Kyrax's swishing blade, threw back his own sword arm, then thrust the blade forwards with all his strength. Metal cut metal and the magical weapon sank deep into the Beast's chest. Tom let go of his sword and fell back, landing in a crouch.

Kyrax lifted a hand, fumbling at

the hilt of the blade lodged in his
heart. His head tipped up, turning
blank eyes to the sky. Then his body
stiffened and started to shake. Tom
heard a terrific, rattling clatter start

up, and realised it was coming from the Beast. Then, suddenly, like a great metal wave breaking, the Beast's body shattered. Tom threw up his arms to protect himself from the metal shards exploding outwards, the sound making the whole city shake. But instead of shards of metal hitting the ground, Tom saw pots and pans, armour and knives, spoons and swords and horseshoes; gold, silver and iron all rained down, bouncing and rolling, tumbling across the cobbles to land in a chaotic glittering pile.

When the din of metal on stone subsided, Tom saw at the heart of the gleaming mess, a small clay figure, no bigger than a cat. Tom's makeshift sword protruded from the statue's chest. But as Tom watched, the sword and the figure crumbled away, leaving nothing but shattered clay and dust. A sudden rush of strength and power flowed over Tom. A warmth like the heat of the sun on a winter's day bathed his tired and aching body.

My Golden Armour! Tom realised. *It's back!*

Tom remembered the fallen soldier.

He scrambled over the pile of stolen treasure, until he came to the prone figure, lying in the shadow of the courtyard wall. Tom leaned over and gently lifted the visor on the brave soldier's dented helmet.

A stab of anguish snatched his breath away. The solider was Elenna!

A huge, swollen purple bruise covered one side of her forehead, her mouth was slack and her eyes were half open, but vacant. Tears sprang to Tom's eyes but he blinked them away. *She can't be dead!* He fumbled for her wrist, clumsy with grief, and felt for a pulse. He waited, trying to still the shuddering inside himself. Panic gripped hold of him. He couldn't feel anything at all...

There! The flicker of a heartbeat, the faintest trace of life. Tom took Epos's talon from his shield and held it to the dark bulge on Elenna's head. The colour faded from the bruise and the swelling vanished. Still Elenna didn't stir. Tom grabbed her wrist again, but her pulse was no stronger. He leaned low over her face, but her breath was too shallow to feel. Tom felt his terrible panic return. He glanced towards Ferno, where the fire dragon lay bleeding on the cobbles nearby.

I can wait, Ferno told him, speaking into his mind through the red jewel.

"I'll be back," Tom said. Then he scooped up Elenna into his arms and ran as fast as he could for the infirmary.

7

ON THE RUN

Candlelight flickered across Elenna's still features as Tom stood at her bedside watching for any sign of change. Daltec had used strong healing magic, and Elenna's breath was sure and steady, but she had still not come around.

"Why doesn't she wake?" Tom asked the young wizard at his side.

It was Aduro who answered from

his chair at the end of the bed.
"Though we have healed the wound,
there may be a permanent injury to
her brain. You must prepare yourself
Tom – not every Quest can have a
happy ending."

Tom heard the chamber door creak
softly open. He looked up to see
Petra hesitate in the doorway, all the
taunting laughter gone from her eyes.

She crossed to Tom's side and gazed
down at Elenna.

"I heard what she did," Petra said.
"You two always have to be too brave
for your own good…" There was a
catch in her voice as she trailed off.
When Tom glanced at the witch, he
saw her eyes shimmering with tears.

Tom took a shuddering breath,

swallowing his own emotion. "If it wasn't for Elenna, the kingdom would have fallen to Kyrax." He gazed down at his friend's pale features and felt a stab of pain in his heart. "Igor will pay for what he has done," he growled.

Tom felt Petra's hand rest on his shoulder. He didn't pull away. There was some comfort in having the witch as his side – knowing she shared his grief. Suddenly Petra gasped and her grip on his shoulder tightened. She pointed at Elenna's hand, where it rested on the bedclothes. In the flickering candlelight, it seemed as still as ever. But then he thought he saw a fingertip twitch. He tried to still the joy rising inside him. *It could just be a trick of the light…* But as he glanced at Elenna's pale face, her eyelids fluttered. He grabbed her hand, hope flooding through him. She opened her eyes and looked up at him, frowning as if the dim light hurt her eyes.

"Where am I?" Elenna croaked.

"Safe in the infirmary," Tom told her, squeezing her palm.

"You hit your head," Petra said helpfully. "Aduro says your brain's been scrambled."

Tom jabbed Petra hard in the ribs. He couldn't help worrying she might be right. But then Elenna's lips twitched into a faint smile.

"Well, at least I've still got a brain," Elenna croaked. "Unlike some people

I could mention."

"Hey!" Petra said, grinning.

Tom felt weak and dizzy with relief. "You had us all worried," he said.

"What happened to Kyrax?" Elenna asked.

"He's nothing more than a pile of pots and pans, thanks to you."

"And Igor is under lock and key," added Petra.

There was a tentative knock on the chamber door. It opened and Captain Harkman strode into the room. The old soldier looked uncomfortable, frowning and shifting his feet, but as his gaze fell on Elenna, he smiled.

"Good to see you awake!" he said. Then his face turned grave again. "Visitors have arrived from the Circle of Wizards. I am afraid they are very insistent that they see Petra at once. They say she must stand trial for stealing the Lightning Staff."

Petra was already halfway across the room. "Ha! Not likely!" she said. "I'm not waiting around to be stripped of my powers like old Aduro over there." She reached the window in three swift steps, and leapt up on to the sill. "See you lot later," she said, then shot Tom a laughing wink, and jumped, vanishing from view.

A few moments later, Tom heard purposeful footsteps striding down the corridor. Captain Harkman stepped aside. A tall, thin witch with high cheekbones and narrow pursed lips bustled into the room, followed by a handful of bearded wizards.

"I have waited long enough," the tall witch snapped. "Where is that treacherous young thief?"

"Can't you see this is a sick room?" Aduro retorted. Elenna let out a long, convincing groan.

"Who are you looking for anyway?"

Tom asked.

The witch's gaze flicked down
to Elenna, then turned back to
Tom, unperturbed. "Petra, of course,"
she said.

Tom shook his head. "Well, she's not
here. We haven't seen her for days."

The tall witch narrowed her eyes

and scanned Tom's face, then turned to study every other face in the chamber. Daltec and Aduro blinked innocently back at her. Captain Harkman lifted his hands.

"As you can see, she isn't here."

The witch gritted her teeth and scowled, but then turned sharply and swept from the room, trailing her long cloak, and her entourage of wizards.

As soon as the chilly click of her footsteps had faded away, Elenna began to laugh – weakly, but the sound filled Tom with joy.

"Do you think they'll find her?" asked Captain Harkman.

"Perhaps one day," said Tom, "but Petra has always been good at looking after herself."

"I'm not sure she'll be welcomed in the Circle of Wizards again, though," said Aduro, chuckling.

Tom grinned. He knew the young witch would be back – the same way that he knew more Beasts would surely threaten Avantia. But for now, his kingdom and friends were safe.

And what could be better than that?

THE END

CONGRATULATIONS, YOU HAVE COMPLETED THIS QUEST!

At the end of each chapter you were awarded a special gold coin. The QUEST in this book was worth an amazing 14 coins.

Look at the Beast Quest totem picture inside the back cover of this book to see how far you've come in your journey to become

MASTER OF THE BEASTS.

The more books you read, the more coins you will collect!

Do you want your own Beast Quest Totem?

1. Cut out and collect the coin below
2. Go to the Beast Quest website
3. Download and print out your totem
4. Add your coin to the totem
www.beastquest.co.uk/totem

CHAPTER ONE

A TERRIBLE HOMECOMING

Tom's body swayed gently in time with Storm's hoofbeats. In the saddle behind him, Elenna let out a contented yawn. Feathery streaks of pink and gold painted the evening sky. The fierce heat of the day had ebbed as they rode. A welcome breeze, sweet with the smell of sun-baked grass, cooled the sweat on Tom's face.

Avantia had been so calm since Tom and Elenna completed their latest Quest that King Hugo had granted them leave to visit Tom's home village, Errinel. Excitement swelled in Tom's chest at the thought of seeing his aunt and uncle again. He spotted a swift shadow loping towards them across the fields. A moment later Silver, Elenna's wolf, took his place at Storm's side.

Read QUARG THE STONE DRAGON to find out more!

Discover the new Beast Quest mobile game from

Available free on iOS and Android

Guide Tom on his Quest to free the Good Beasts
of Avantia from Malvel's evil spells.

Battle the Beasts, defeat the minions,
unearth the secrets and collect
rewards as you journey through the
Kingdom of Avantia.

DOWNLOAD THE APP TO BEGIN
THE ADVENTURE NOW!

MAR 2017